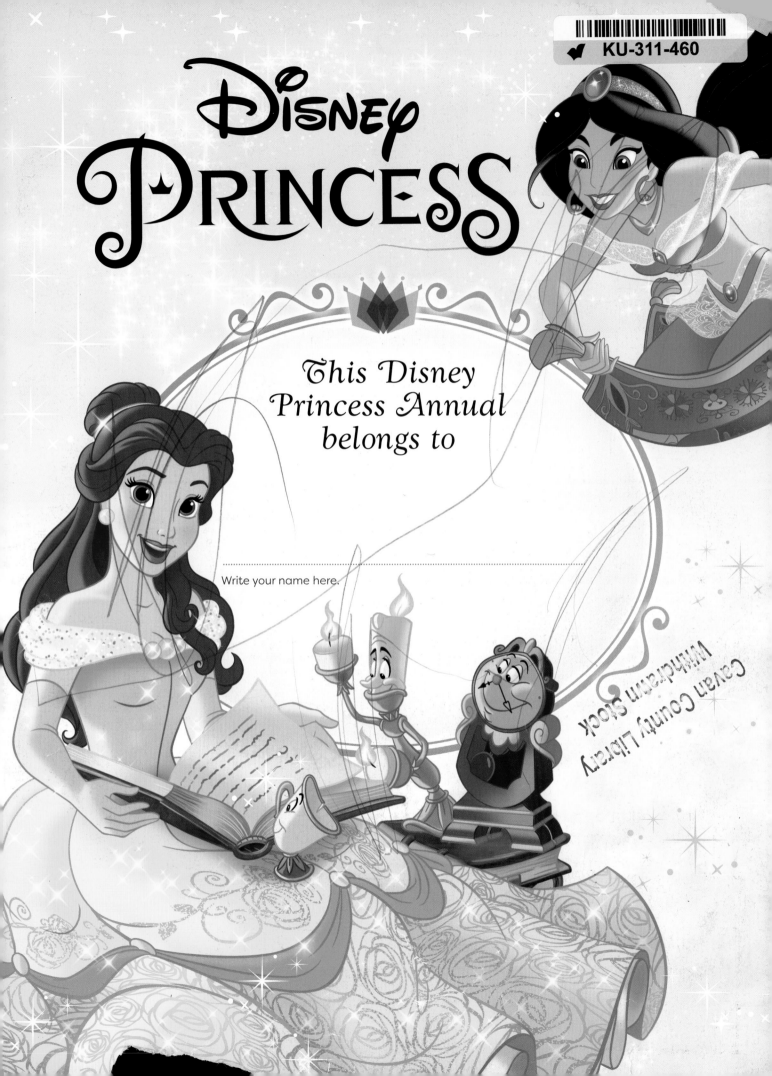

DISNEY PRINCESS

This Disney Princess Annual belongs to

....

Write your name here.

Disney PRINCESS

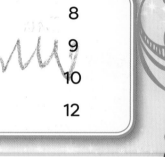

EGMONT
We bring stories to life

First published in Great Britain in 2019
by Egmont UK Limited,
The Yellow Building, 1 Nicholas Road, London W11 4AN

Content written and adapted by Jude Exley
Designed by Thelma-Jane Robb

© 2019 Disney Enterprises, Inc.

The movie THE PRINCESS AND THE FROG copyright © 2009, Disney,
inspired in part by the book THE FROG PRINCESS by E. D. Baker
copyright © 2002, published by Bloomsbury Publishing, Inc.

ISBN 978 1 4052 9442 3
70374/003
Printed in Italy

Parental guidance is advised for all craft and colouring activities.
Always ask an adult to help when using glue, paint and scissors.
Wear protective clothes and cover surfaces to avoid damage or staining.

Stay safe online. Egmont is not responsible for content
hosted by third parties.

Egmont takes its responsibility to the planet and its inhabitants
very seriously. We aim to use paper from well-managed forests
run by responsible suppliers.

Turn the page and let the adventures begin ...

Meet Jasmine

- Jasmine is the daughter of the Sultan of Agrabah.

- She is independent and won't hesitate to stand up for what's right.

- When she meets Aladdin, she discovers the wonder and adventure she'd often imagined outside the palace walls.

- Jasmine is kind-hearted and cares a great deal about her kingdom, her family and her friends.

- She loves her pet tiger, Rajah, who is a loyal friend.

"You're not gonna find another girl like her in a million years."

– GENIE TO ALADDIN, ABOUT JASMINE

Flying High

Colour in Jasmine on the magic carpet using the smaller picture to help you.

Clever Kitty

One day, Jasmine and Aladdin were watching a circus parade. There were jugglers, elephants and even trained tigers who could balance fruit on their noses! Jasmine's tiger, Rajah, tried to join in, but he put the tigers off their act and all the pieces of fruit went crashing to the ground!

"You'd need a lot of practice to do their trick," Jasmine told Rajah.

On the walk home, Rajah stopped in front of a fruit stall in the market and looked longingly at its display.

"I think Rajah really does want to learn the tigers' tricks," said Aladdin.

Jasmine agreed. She bought lots and lots of melons and brought them back to the palace.

Jasmine helped Rajah try to balance fruit on his nose. They soon discovered that balancing melons was a lot harder than it looked. Rajah must have dropped them at least a hundred times!

"Practice makes perfect," Jasmine would say each time Rajah dropped a melon, propping it back onto his nose.

They practised all week until Rajah could balance a melon on the tip of his nose just like the parading tigers. But Rajah wanted to be even better than those tigers, so next he tried to balance two melons. It was twice as hard! So you can only imagine how much harder it was to balance three melons!

WRITE in the missing numbers for Rajah's steps.

Rajah never gave up and, with enough practice, he learned to balance three melons on his nose. When the parade leader visited again, Jasmine showed him Rajah's trick.

"I've never seen anything like it," the parade leader exclaimed. "You should be at the front of my parade!"

So, for one day only, Princess Jasmine and her very clever kitty led the parade through the town!

The End

Garden Party

Jasmine is hosting a feast at the palace for the local children!

It's very busy in the kitchen as everyone helps to prepare the food.

1 **SPOT** the baker putting bread in the oven.

2 How many bread rolls can you **COUNT**?

WRITE your answer here.

3 **JOIN** the dots using the same colour to finish the fruit. Can you **NAME** each fruit?

4

The feast is ready. **TICK** the food you like best!

5 **FIND** these details and **COLOUR** in the frames when you do.

Answers on page 69.

Meet Belle

- Belle lives in a little French village with her inventor father, Maurice.

- She is intelligent and her love of books has given her a great imagination and open mind.

- When she meets the Beast, her bravery and compassion enable her to break the curse and restore love and laughter to the castle.

- Belle isn't afraid to be different and fight for what's right.

- The enchanted objects, including Lumière, Cogsworth, Mrs Potts and Chip, are Belle's friends.

"She warned him not to be deceived by appearances, for beauty is found within."

NARRATOR

Belle's Friends

Can you match Lumière, Cogsworth,
Mrs Potts and Chip to their shadows?

The Gift Hunt

1 It was Belle's birthday, but her father, Maurice, was a little behind schedule and her gift wasn't ready yet.

2 So he hurried into the village where the baker, the bookseller and the flower girl all agreed to help send Belle on a hunt for her gift! This would give Maurice time to finish it.

It's a treasure hunt
So look for your clue
In a village store
That's special to you

3 Back home, Maurice explained to Belle that she would need to hunt for her gift this year and handed her the first clue!

4 Belle thought for a minute. Then she raced to the village bookshop, but the bookseller wouldn't let her in. "Wait ..." he said. "I ... um ... I am washing the floors."

Is Belle's gift ready?
TICK your answer.

yes   no

16

5 "But, I need to get my clue!" said Belle puzzled, not knowing he was really trying to slow her down so Maurice would have more time to finish her gift!

On this treasure hunt
You haven't strayed
So find your next clue
Where bread is made

6 Belle waited impatiently until the bookseller finally gave her the next clue. Then she raced through the village to ...

 2 What **COLOUR** are the raspberries on the cake?

8 Just when she couldn't wait any longer, the baker finally gave Belle her next clue:

7 ... the village bakery! Belle had to wait until the baker finished a cake. "It looks lovely now," she said. "Can I have my clue?" "No, it still needs more raspberries," replied the baker.

Flowers of reds
and golds
Plus your clue
she holds
To lead you to
your gift
Hurry Belle,
be swift

Answers on page 69.

9 "The flower girl must have my next clue!" said Belle and she hurried to her stand by the fountain. She could see the flower girl holding a clue.

3

COLOUR in the pretty flowers.

10 But when Belle reached the flower girl, she made Belle chase her to get the clue. When Belle finally caught her, the last clue directed Belle right back home!

11 There Maurice explained everything to Belle, and she laughed when she finally understood why everyone had acted so strangely!

12 Then Maurice led Belle to her gift. "Oh, thank you, Father!" said Belle. "It's the perfect reading chair!"

13 Later, Maurice's helpers all came to help celebrate Belle's birthday. Of course, everyone had to try out the new chair!

The End

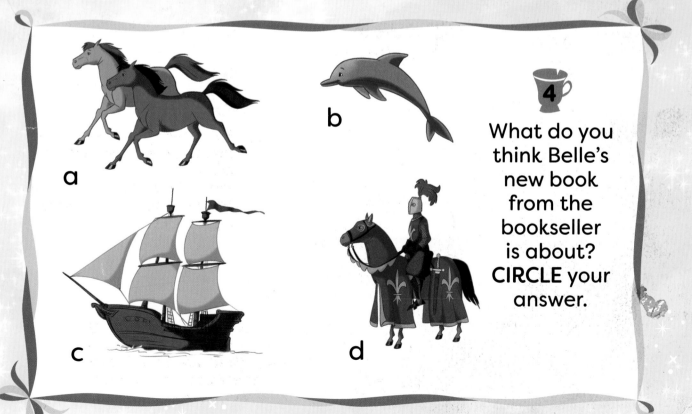

a

b

c

d

4 What do you think Belle's new book from the bookseller is about? CIRCLE your answer.

B is for Belle

Belle's name begins with the letter 'b'.
Have fun with these alphabet activities.

1

TRACE the letters to write 'Belle'.

Belle

2

CROSS out the letters which appear three times to reveal Belle's favourite things.

n d n v d e
a b o o k s a
v a e d v n e

3

Can you **FILL IN** the missing letters of the alphabet?

a ☐ c d ☐ f g h ☐

Answers on page 69.

Belle's Rose

There are many different flowers, but the rose is Belle's favourite!

1 **ADD** up these flower sums.

a  **+**  **=**

b  **+** **=**

c  **+** **=**

2 **FINISH** the colour sequence below.

3 **COLOUR** Lumière and **TRACE** his flames.

Answers on page 69.

Meet Cinderella

- Cinderella lives with her cruel stepmother and selfish stepsisters in a French chateau.

- She is hard-working, humble and kind, despite her step family's cruelty.

- When Cinderella goes to the royal ball, thanks to her Fairy Godmother, her life is changed forever and she can live her dreams.

- Cinderella is optimistic and has faith that if you keep on believing, your wish will come true.

- The birds and mice, including Jaq and Gus, are Cinderella's loyal friends and helpers.

"Oh, it's a beautiful dress! And look! Glass slippers. Why, it's like a dream. A wonderful dream come true."

– CINDERELLA

Cinderella's Helpers

Cinderella has some loyal little animal friends!

1

SPOT the odd one out in each row.

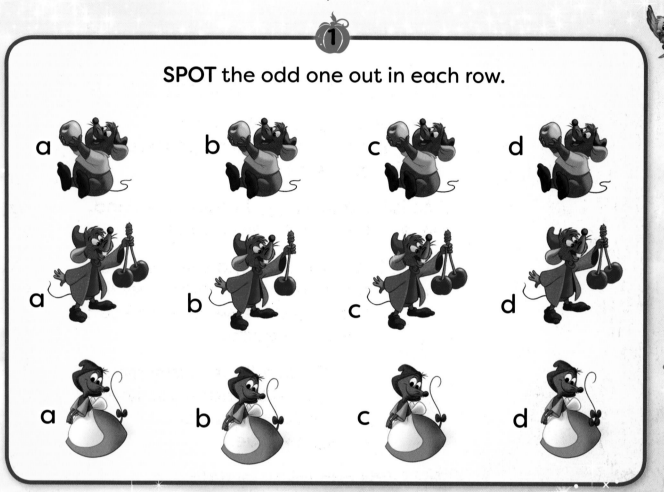

a   b   c   d

a   b   c   d

a   b   c   d

2

Put these pictures of Gus in **ORDER**, starting with the smallest one.

a   b   c   d

| 1 | | | |

3

COUNT the little birds and circle the correct number.

5   6

Abraca-Lucifer!

One day, the Fairy Godmother was washing her wand when Lucifer sneaked up to the washing bowl and started to drink from it.

"Lucifer, stop it!" the Fairy Godmother scolded. "Some of the magic from my wand will have washed into the water!"

Just then Lucifer saw Jaq and Gus and began to chase them. But suddenly he sneezed and a very strange thing happened ... a bolt of lightning zapped from his nose and burned a mark on the floor!

Ka-zap!

He sneezed again and more magical bolts of lightning fired from his nose!

"Lucifer's got magic powers!" Gus wailed. Lucifer laughed as the mice ran away to hide under Cinderella's bed. Knowing he could zap the mice at any time,

SHOUT the word Ka-zap in the story.

24

Lucifer decided to check his bowl for food. But then ...

Ka-zap!

... he sneezed again and his bowl was zapped by lightning! Lucifer got a bit scared so he decided to rest in his basket. But before he could hold another sneeze back ...

Ka-zap!

... he had zapped his favourite blanket with lightning, too!

Lucifer was very scared now. What if he could never control his magic powers?

A little later, Cinderella found a very worried Lucifer hiding under her bed. Gus and Jaq were dancing with joy on top of it. "What are you all doing?" she asked.

"Lucifer drank magic water," Gus laughed, "and now he can't stop z-z-zapping things!"

Cinderella took Lucifer to the Fairy Godmother, who used a spell to stop his magic lightning bolts forever.

"I did warn you about the magic water!" the Fairy Godmother said. Lucifer had learned his lesson ... magic was for fairies, not cats!

The End

Magical Moment

Cinderella will go to the ball - with the help
of some Fairy Godmother magic!

1 **SPOT** the six differences
between the two pictures.

a

2

CIRCLE the mouse who is **NOT** in the pictures.

a

b

c

d

Answers on page 69.

COLOUR in a glass slipper each time you find a difference.

b

4

WHICH path leads Gus to Jaq?

a

b

c

Meet Mulan

- Mulan is the daughter of Fa Zhou, a renowned war hero.

- She is fearless and determined, despite how her family expect her to behave.

- When she disguises herself as a man and joins the Chinese Imperial Army in her father's place, she becomes a hero for helping to defeat the Hun.

- Mulan is intelligent and resourceful, using her quick thinking and military skills to earn her place in the army amongst the men.

- Cri-kee, Mushu and Khan are her faithful friends.

"The greatest gift and honour is having you for a daughter."

– FA ZHOU, MULAN'S FATHER

Maze to Khan

Can you help Mulan through the maze to reach Khan?

Start

Finish

Dragon Breath

One warm summer's day, Mushu the dragon was cooling off at the stream. He ducked his head under the water and gargled —

"Glug-glug-glug-glug!"

— until he felt refreshed. Then, Mushu ran to help Mulan with her warrior training.

Mushu would normally breathe fireballs for Mulan to dodge but today, the only thing that came out of Mushu's mouth was a long trail of bubbles!

"Where's my fire?" Mushu wailed. He tried again, but this time he just got hiccups! "I can't be a dragon if I can't breathe fire!"

Mulan knew what it was like when people doubted you — no one had believed she could be a warrior — so she knew just how to help Mushu.

"Instead of fireballs, let's try jogging," she said.

Mushu and Mulan jogged around the garden. When they got back to the house, Mushu was full of energy while Mulan pretended to stop for a drink. "You're much better than me at keeping cool," Mulan said.

"I suppose I am," Mushu said.

"But can you defend yourself against a true warrior?" Mulan asked, drawing her sword.

Without thinking, Mushu breathed a string of fireballs that lit up the whole garden! "Hey, my fire!" Mushu said. "It's back! Guess I'm not such a poor dragon after all."

Mulan gave Mushu a hug. "That's what I knew all along!" she said.

The End

1

COUNT how many bubbles Mushu has blown.

2

POINT to Cri-Kee in the picture.

Answers on page 69.

Fun with Mulan

Have fun solving these puzzles with Mulan and her friends!

1

NUMBER the sections below from 1 to 6 to put them in the correct order.

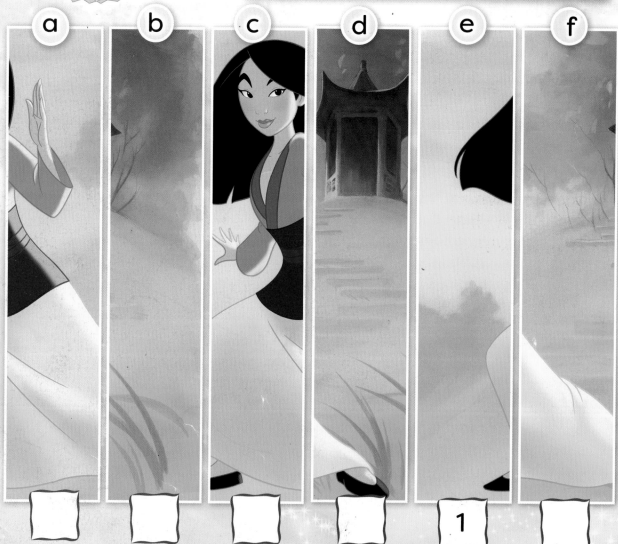

a   b   c   d   e   f

[ ]   [ ]   [ ]   [ ]   [1]   [ ]

2 MATCH these friends with their shadows.

a

b

c

1

2

3

3 WHICH path leads Mulan to her horse, Khan?

c

b

a

4 COLOUR in the flag when you've finished the activities.

Meet Rapunzel

- Rapunzel lives in a tall tower with Gothel who kidnapped her when she was a child.

- She is full of curiosity about the world and believes her true destiny lies outside the tower walls.

- When she meets Flynn, she leaves the tower for the first time and discovers a long-hidden secret and the strength to fulfil her dreams.

- Rapunzel is spirited and determined to experience life to the full, enjoying art and music and finding beauty in all she sees.

- Pascal, her faithful chameleon, loves to be by her side.

"I am the lost princess, aren't I?"

– RAPUNZEL TO GOTHEL

Chameleon Colours

Rapunzel and Pascal have some fun colour puzzles for you to solve.

1

CIRCLE the **GREEN** Pascal.

a    b    c    d

2

TICK the **PURPLE** dress.

a   b   c   d

3

Which colour comes next in each sequence? **COLOUR** your answer.

a

b

c

Hidden Treasure

I love dancing!

1 One afternoon Rapunzel and Pascal were having a great time dancing around the tower. "This is so much fun!" cried Rapunzel as she did a twirl.

1

FOLLOW the twirling trail to dance around the tower with Rapunzel and Pascal.

2 But suddenly Rapunzel felt the bracelet she was wearing snap and fall to the ground. It disappeared between a crack in the floorboards.

Oh no!

3 Rapunzel got down on her hands and knees to look for the bracelet but all she could see was darkness. "It's gone forever," she sighed sadly.

4 Rapunzel didn't feel like dancing any more, so she found a book about a pirate adventure. "Why don't we make up our own pirate adventure?" she suggested to Pascal.

Let's be pirates, me hearty!

2

a   b   c

CIRCLE the book that matches the one Rapunzel is reading.

5 Rapunzel made pirate hats, built a pirate ship and drew a treasure map. Then she hid buttons for Pascal to find. "X marks the spot," she told her friend, giving him the map.

Can you find the treasure, shipmate?

6 But Pascal wasn't very good at map reading! Instead, he rushed around the tower pulling everything apart! He found plenty of missing items and eventually uncovered the treasure.

Answers on page 69.

7 Looking at the things Pascal had found gave Rapunzel an idea and she used the treasure to make a new bracelet. "It's nice," Rapunzel sighed, "but I still miss my old one."

8 Soon it began to get dark and Rapunzel lit a candle. The flame shone on her new bracelet making the buttons shine. "Maybe I can find my old bracelet after all!" she exclaimed.

9 Rapunzel held the candle over the crack in the floorboards and her missing bracelet sparkled in the light. With the help of a hastily-made tool she tried to fish it out ...

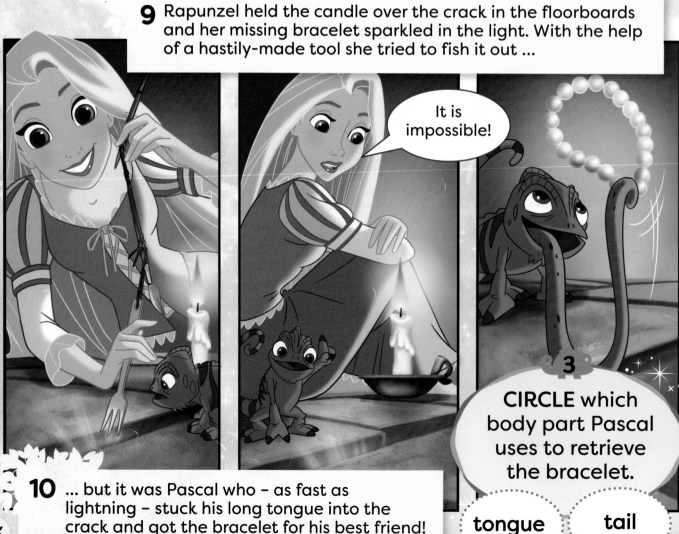

It is impossible!

3

CIRCLE which body part Pascal uses to retrieve the bracelet.

tongue   tail

10 ... but it was Pascal who – as fast as lightning – stuck his long tongue into the crack and got the bracelet for his best friend!

11 Rapunzel was overjoyed! "Thanks to you Pascal, I've got my old bracelet back and I've got a new one. You really are the best at finding treasure!"

Shiver me timbers, that was fun!

The End

CIRCLE the pirate object which is not in the picture.

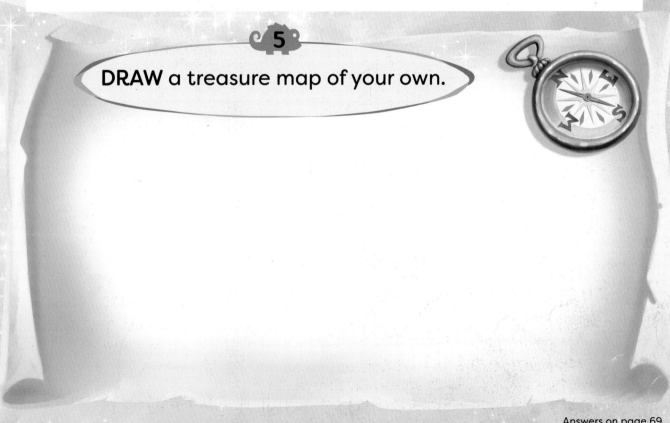

DRAW a treasure map of your own.

39

Colourful Craft

Here's how to make a rainbow scratchboard to create beautiful artwork - just like Rapunzel!

You will need:

- Stiff white card
- Coloured pencils
- Black wax crayon
- Paintbrush

1

COLOUR rainbow stripes on to the card with your coloured pencils.

2

USE the black crayon to colour a layer of black over the top of the rainbow colours.

TIP: Try to make the black layer as thick as possible!

3

With the pointed handle end of the paintbrush **SCRATCH** away the black crayon to reveal the rainbow colours underneath.

4

CREATE pretty patterns or **DRAW** colourful pictures onto your scratchboard.

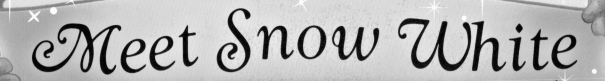

Meet Snow White

- Snow White lives with her wicked stepmother, the Evil Queen, until her life is in danger.

- She is kind and optimistic, despite being made to work as a maid for her stepmother.

- When she meets the Seven Dwarfs, her troubles are not over, but her pure heart ultimately saves her life.

- Snow White is charming and maternal, quickly winning the trust and admiration of the Seven Dwarfs and the Prince.

- The forest animals and the Seven Dwarfs are her devoted friends.

"Lips red as the rose, hair black as ebony, skin white as snow."

– MAGIC MIRROR

Who's Who?

Draw a line to match the correct Dwarfs to the smaller pictures below.

Doc

Grumpy

Happy

Sneezy

Dopey

Bashful

Sleepy

1

2

3

4

5

6

7

A Colourful Surprise

1 It was a warm, bright day and Snow White and the Dwarfs were baking lots of food to take on a picnic.

It smells lovely!

2 "This will be fun!" cheered Happy, as he helped Snow White pack the picnic basket. "Eating inside would be easier," grumbled Grumpy.

1

CIRCLE the items that are in the picnic basket.

Answers on page 69.

3 Just as Snow White and the Dwarfs were about to leave the cottage, dark clouds appeared in the sky and it started to rain.

4 "I knew eating outside would be trouble," moaned Grumpy.

5 But luckily, Snow White had a plan. "We can have our picnic inside instead," she said.

6 Snow White laid the picnic blanket on the floor in the kitchen and they unpacked the food. "Thanks for saving our picnic," said Happy.

2

WRITE how many apples you can see in picture 6.

7 Snow White and the Dwarfs eagerly tucked into their feast, but Grumpy still had a frown on his face.

8 Just then, the dark clouds cleared. "The sun's coming out!" cried Happy.

9 Everyone gasped as a colourful rainbow appeared in the sky. "This is the most beautiful picnic we've ever had," said Snow White. Even Grumpy had to agree!

The End

3 SPOT these items in the picture above.

4 COLOUR the rainbow.

Dwarfs and Apples

Lead the Dwarfs home to Snow White in this fun game.

You will need: A counter for each player and a dice.

33 34 35 36

32 31 30 29

17 18 19 20

16 15 14 13

1 Start 2 3 4

HOW TO PLAY:

Take turns to roll the dice and move your counter forward the number of spaces shown. If you land on a Dwarf, follow the arrow to jump upwards. If your counter lands on an apple, you must drop down the arrow. The first to reach Snow White wins!

40

37

38

39

Finish

28

27

26

25

21

22

23

24

12

11

10

9

5

6

7

8

Meet Ariel

- Ariel lives in the kingdom of Atlantica with her father, King Triton.

- She is bright and spirited with a passion for exploration and adventure.

- When she explores the world beyond the ocean, she sacrifices all things dear to her for her true love.

- Ariel is very caring and protective, willing to risk her own life for her friends.

- Her closest friends are Flounder and Sebastian.

"I don't see how a world that makes such wonderful things could be bad."

— ARIEL

Finding Friends

Can you help Ariel work out which line she should follow to find her friends?

a

b

c

The Helpful Daughter

Ariel and her sisters had practised all month to perform at the royal gala. "I hope Daddy likes our song," said Adella.

But as the sisters began, a terrible noise drowned them out ...

Zzzzzzzzzzzz!

King Triton was fast asleep and his snoring was echoing through the whole room! The sisters were disappointed, but Ariel realised that the king had fallen asleep because he had been working so hard. So, the next day, Ariel asked if she could help her father in his royal duties. "I can help organise and do anything you need me to," she insisted.

"I suppose I could do with some help to make sure my guests' visits run smoothly," the King admitted.

For the rest of the day, Ariel met every merperson who came to see the king, and found out as much as she could about them before they saw him.

When they met the king, Ariel had already told him why they were there and what they wanted, so King Triton could deal with everyone quickly and fairly.

Ariel was so helpful that King Triton asked her to do it again the next day. And the next! And the next! "You've shown great thoughtfulness in helping me when I needed you," King Triton said. "As a reward, I would like you to help host our next royal gala."

"Really?!" Ariel asked. She was thrilled! Ariel helped host the next gala with her father, as well as singing there with her sisters. In fact, she worked so hard, no one could blame her when ...

Zzzzzzzzzzz!

This time it was Ariel who fell asleep, just before dessert was served!

The End

WHICH coloured note appears the most often?

53

Seashell Search

Join Ariel and her friends by playing a game of three-in-a-row.

1 Which seashell needs to be added to make three-in-a-row? **DRAW** it in the correct square.

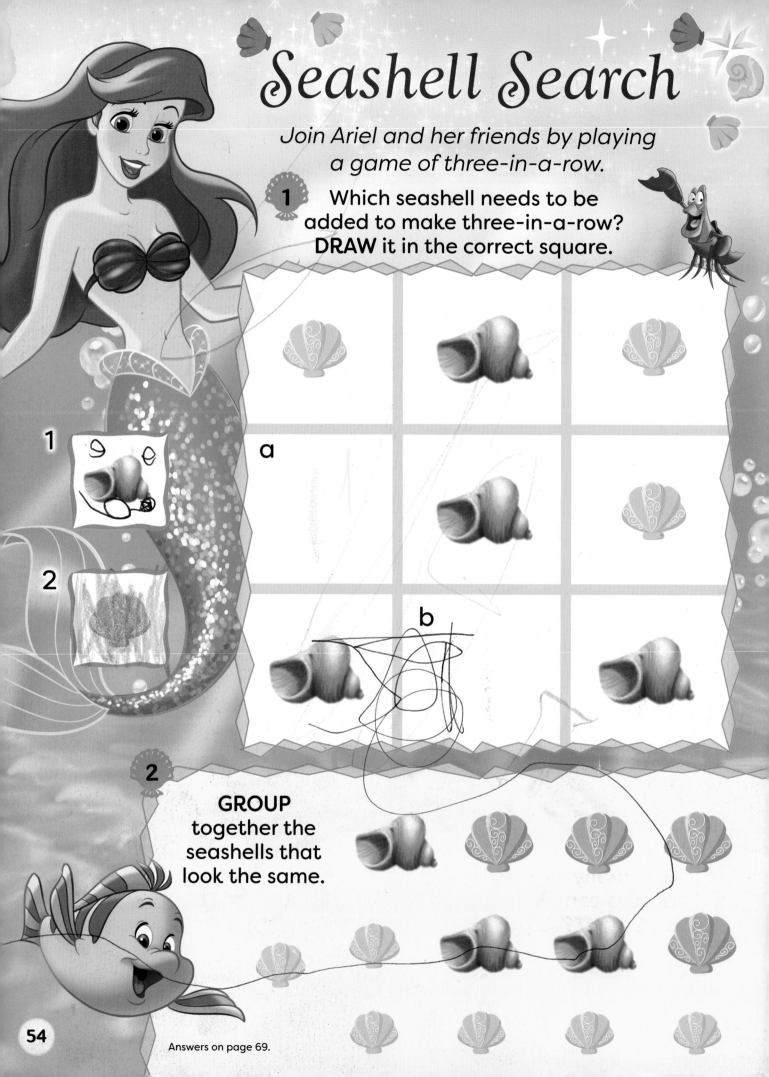

a

b

1

2

2

GROUP together the seashells that look the same.

Answers on page 69.

Underwater Fun

Ariel and Flounder are enjoying spinning around in the deep blue sea.

1

Add some **COLOUR** to the underwater friends to finish this picture.

2

Sebastian is hiding. Can you **FIND** him?

3

How many bubbles can you **COUNT?**

Answers on page 69.

Meet Tiana

- Tiana lives In New Orleans near her wealthy friend, Charlotte.

- She is intelligent, resourceful and a gifted chef and business woman.

- When Tiana changes into a frog, she goes on an unexpected adventure that proves she should never be underestimated.

- Tiana is a firm believer in hard work, but is also passionate and imaginative, valuing music and time with loved ones.

- Tiana's animal friend turns out to be a prince!

"The only way that you can get what you want in this world is through hard work."

— TIANA

Creative Cooking

Tiana loves cooking with lots of colourful fruit and vegetables.

1

COLOUR Tiana's clothes in your favourite colours.

2

CIRCLE all the red food you can spot.

3

Can you NAME and colour these vegetables?

c _____

t _____

p _____

Tiana's Palace

1 One day, Tiana learned that the city's sternest food critic was reviewing restaurants in the area. "Don't be nervous, Tiana," said Prince Naveen. "The critic will see just how great Tiana's Palace is."

2 That very evening, the critic showed up at Tiana's Palace and surprised them.

COLOUR in the flowers to help Tiana make the restaurant extra pretty.

3 "This is a special night," Tiana explained as Eudora and Charlotte helped the critic into a ballgown, gloves and tiara. But the critic didn't look impressed.

2 **CIRCLE** the things the critic is wearing.

a

b

c

d

4 When the critic was shown to her seat in the dining area, she looked like a princess. She gasped when she saw that everyone else was dressed like royalty, too.

5 Once all the guests were seated, Tiana led everyone in a toast. "Welcome to our monthly Royal Night at Tiana's Palace," she said, and everyone cheered.

6 The critic was pleasantly surprised that she did not receive any special treatment from Tiana. She could see that everyone was treated equally well at Tiana's Palace.

7 All guests were served the finest food and every dish followed one of Tiana's delicious recipes.

3 Help the band play some swinging music by **MATCHING** the notes into pairs.

8 The critic could not resist a dance before the night was over. "I think she likes Tiana's Palace," Prince Naveen said to Tiana, "just like everyone who visits!"

9 The critic had never had such a lovely time and she didn't want to leave. "What a magical place," she sighed, as she went home.

10 The critic's review gave Tiana's Palace top marks and described it as "A royal place where everyone will be treated as a prince or princess".

Tiana's Palace

1 2 3 4 5

4

COUNT how many stars Tiana's Palace was given. Then **TRACE** the numbers and the stars.

1 2 3 4 5

11 And that is exactly how everyone feels when they come to eat at Tiana's restaurant!

The End

Meet Aurora

- Aurora is the daughter of King Stefan and Queen Leah, but she lives with Flora, Fauna and Merryweather to escape Maleficent's curse.

- She is gentle and loyal to her aunts, even when she doesn't agree with them.

- On her christening day, Aurora was cursed by Maleficent to a doomed future, and lives in hiding, until her true fate is revealed.

- Aurora is a hopeless romantic who is delighted when her betrothed and true love are the same person.

- She sings and dances with her woodland animal friends.

"They say if you dream a thing, more than once, it's sure to come true."

- AURORA

Fairy Fun

Can you help Aurora solve these fun puzzles?

1

WHICH fairy comes next in this sequence?

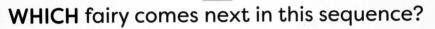

a   b   c   a   b

2

CIRCLE the odd fairy out?

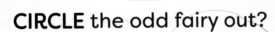

a   b   c   d

3

FIND Merryweather's shadow.

a   b   c

Answers on page 69.

Juggling Molly

1 Aurora loved her life in the palace, but sometimes she liked to put on a simple dress and walk to the village. Often, no one recognised her. On one such walk, Aurora saw a young girl juggling three balls!

3 Molly decided to train Aurora with scarves as they were much easier to catch. Aurora was getting better at juggling! Molly invited her to a picnic with her new friends the next day.

2 The girl was called Molly and she didn't know that Aurora was a princess. She offered to teach Aurora how to juggle. But juggling wasn't as easy as it looked.

4 When Aurora arrived at the picnic, the village girls began to bow and curtsey. "Oh, sorry, I didn't know ..." said Molly, feeling embarrassed. But Aurora knew the picnic was meant to be for Molly, so she tossed her some apples to juggle.

5 The village girls were amazed by Molly and seemed to forget all about the princess in their midst. Aurora was delighted to see Molly shine in front of her new friends.

The End

Woodland Colours

The fairy godmothers are giving Aurora's dress a makeover using the colours of the forest.

1

ADD woodland colours to Aurora's dress.

2

These leaves have beautiful colours. **MATCH** the pairs.

3

Which leaf has no match? **CIRCLE** it.

Answers on page 69.

Disney
PRINCESS

DISNEY PRINCESS

Thanks for joining us!
We'll see you again
in next year's
Disney Princess
Annual!

Answers

Pages 12-13 *Garden Party -*

1)

2) 9 bread rolls.

3) banana, apple, pear

5)

Page 15 *Belle's Friends*

a-4, b-2, c-3, d-1.

Pages 16-19 *The Gift Hunt*

1) no.

2) red.

4) a.

Page 20 *B is for Belle*

2) books.

3) b, e, i.

Page 21 *Belle's Rose*

1) a=9, b=5, c=8.

2)

Page 23 *Cinders' Helpers*

1) c, b, d.

2) a, c, b, d.

3) 6.

Page 26 *Magical Moment*

1)

2) b.

4) b.

Page 29 *Maze to Khan*

Pages 30-31 *Dragon Breath*

1) 6.

Page 32 *Fun with Mulan*

1) 1 - e, 2 - c, 3 - a, 4 - f,

5 - d, 6 - b.

2) a - 2, b - 3, c - 1.

3) c.

Page 35 *Chameleon Colours*

1) b.

2) c.

3) a-purple, b-blue, c-green.

Pages 36-39 *Hidden Treasure*

2) c. 3) tongue. 4) hat.

Page 43 *Who's Who?*

1) Doc-3, Grumpy-5, Happy-2

Sneezy-6, Dopey-4, Bashful-1,

Sleepy-7

Pages 44-47 *Colourful Surprise*

1)

2) 8.

3)

Page 51 *Finding Friends*

c.

Pages 52-53 *The Helpful Daughter*

Dark blue.

Page 54 *Seashell Search*

1) b.

2)

Page 55 *Underwater Fun*

2)

3) There are 8 bubbles.

Page 57 *Creative Cooking*

2)

3) carrot, tomato, pepper

Pages 58-61 *Tiana's Palace*

2) a and c.

3)

Page 63 *Fairy Fun*

1) c.

2) c.

3) c.

Page 66 *Woodland Colours*

2)

3)